WE CAN READ!™

Critter Sitters

by Jacqueline Sweeney

photography by G. K. & Vikki Hart
photo illustration by Blind Mice Studio

BENCHMARK **B**OOKS

MARSHALL CAVENDISH
NEW YORK

For Sarina, Matthew, Theo, Gabby, and Avra, who will always exhaust us with the incredible momentum of their lives.

With thanks to Daria Murphy, reading specialist and principal of Scotchtown Elementary, Goshen, New York, for reading this manuscript with care and for writing the "We Can Read and Learn" activity guide.

Benchmark Books
Marshall Cavendish
99 White Plains Road
Tarrytown, New York 10591-9001
Website:www.marshallcavendish.com

Text copyright © 2002 by Jacqueline Sweeney
Photo illustrations © 2002 by G.K. & Vikki Hart
and Mark and Kendra Empey

Library of Congress Cataloging-in-Publication Data
Sweeney, Jacqueline.
Critter Sitters /by Jacqueline Sweeney.
p.   cm. — (We can read!)
Summary: Animal friends help each other out by babysitting six little mice on a wintry day.
ISBN 0-7614-1122-4
[1. Mice—Fiction. 2. Animals—Infancy—Fiction. 3. Babysitting—Fiction.] I. Title.
PZ7.S974255 Ct 2001   [E]—dc21   00-046866

Printed in Italy

1 3 5 6 4 2

Characters

Milly

Clem

Molly

Gus

Hildy

Jim

Ladybug

Tim

Ron

Eddie

The Boys

"I want to go," said Milly.

"We can't go," said Clem.

"I know," sniffed Milly.

"Go where, big sister?" asked Molly.

"To a wedding," said Milly.

"But we can't leave the boys."

"I'll watch them!" said Molly.

"I'll help," said Gus.

"Are you sure?" asked Clem.

"There are six of them!"

"That's a lot of mice," said Gus.

"We'll need help."

Molly told Hildy.

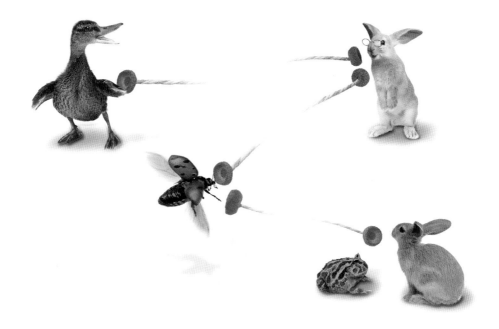

Hildy told Jim.

Jim told Ladybug.

She told Ron and Tim.

"Wake up, Eddie!" yelled Molly.

"It's time to critter sit."

"Meet Hank, Clyde, Curly, Ollie,
Pip, and Blinky," said Milly.
"When do they eat?" asked Molly.
"When do they *sleep*?" asked Gus.

Clem gave Gus a long list.

"It's all here," he said.

"See you in three days."

Blinky started to cry,

then Ollie, then Pip.

"What do we do?" asked Gus.

"Hug them!" said Molly.

"Then take them to the pond."

Hildy found six scarves.

Ron found six hats.

13

Soon six mice were skating.

They threw snowballs.

They made snow critters.

It was getting late.

"Time to go home!" said Molly.

"NO!" squeaked Hank.

He ran under a rock.

"NO!" squeaked Ollie.

He ran into the woods.

Pip and Blinky climbed a tree.

Clyde and Curly cried.

It took a long time to get home.

Six tired mice had supper.

22

Six tired mice had baths.

Eddie told a story.

Hildy sang a song.

Ollie yawned,

Then Hank,

Then Pip,

Then Blinky,

Then Clyde.

Curly started snoring.

So did Ron.

"What shall we do tomorrow?" asked Molly.

But no one said a word.

WE CAN READ AND LEARN

The following activities are designed to enhance literacy development. *Critter Sitters* can help children to build skills in vocabulary, phonics, and creative writing; to explore self-awareness; and to make connections between literature and other subject areas, such as science and math.

THE SITTERS' CHALLENGE WORDS

There are many challenging vocabulary words in this story. After discussing each word's meaning, have children write each word on an index card and sort the words in a variety of ways. For example, sort action words (verbs) and nouns; sort one-, two-, or three-syllable words; sort words with similar suffixes (-ed, -ing, -s).

watch	leave	wedding	list
scarves	found	skating	long
snowballs	climbed	yawned	supper
snoring	tomorrow	word	baths

FUN WITH PHONICS

Oh, no! There's so much snow!
Help children to identify all the long o words in this story. Cut out construction paper snowballs and write the words on them. Find the similar word patterns, as listed below. Use these words to write a story about how to spend a snowy day. Add more long o words if you can.

go	snow	home	so
no	know	dove (He dove into the snow.)	

BEDTIME STORIES

The critter sitters know how important it is to share bedtime with a story, a lullaby, or a hug. Whether at home or at school, the idea of a bedtime (or a rest-time) story can strengthen listening skills and be a calming and peaceful experience. Share your favorite bedtime story from your own childhood.

Have children write stories about a time when they took care of someone or something, the way the critter sitters took such good care of the six little mice. What would they do? Children can also write stories about the importance of caring. Write about ways we can show that we care about each other, our families, our Earth.

Everyone needs a hug sometimes. Have each child lie down on a sheet of paper as wide as his or her arms when they are spread out. With a pencil, draw along the length of the child's arms. Help the child to cut along the pencil line, from hand to hand, to create a paper hug that can be wrapped around someone who needs one. Write a special, loving phrase or message on the paper hug and send it to a loved one who is far way.

SIX HATS, SIX MICE, SIX SCARVES, HOW NICE

Help children to explore number concepts. Create a number book using objects, animals, and other things from the story. On each page, write the number and the number words and draw or glue pictures to represent that numeral concept. For example:

1	2
one	two
Y	Y Y

SNOWFLAKES AND NAMES, BOTH SPECIAL AND UNIQUE

There are many characters in this story, each with a special name. Just as each snowflake is special, so is a person's name. Help children to cut out snowflakes by folding white paper squares in half and then in quarters. Cut out shapes and notches and unfold a unique snowflake. Children can write their names on the snowflakes. Research the meaning of each name and record the information on the other side. Cut out snowflakes for each member of the children's families, so that they can have their own little "snowstorms."

CREATIVE WRITING

What shall we do tomorrow? Have children answer this simple question by writing about their own lives or a new day of adventures for the six little mice and their Critter Sitters.

31

About the author

Jacqueline Sweeney is a poet and children's author. She has worked with children and teachers for over twenty-five years implementing writing workshops in schools throughout the United States. She specializes in motivating reluctant writers and shares her creative teaching methods in numerous professional books for teachers. She lives in Stone Ridge, New York.

About the photo illustrations

The photo illustrations are the collaborative effort of photographers G. K. and Vikki Hart and Blind Mice Studio. Following Mark Empey's sketched storyboard, G. K. and Vikki Hart photograph each animal and element individually. The images are then scanned and manipulated, pixel by pixel, by Mark and Kendra Empey at Blind Mice Studio.

Each charming illustration may contain from 15 to 30 individual photographs.

All the animals that appear in this book were handled with love. They have been returned to or adopted by loving homes.